QUICKREADS

THE WOMAN WHO LOVED A GHOST

JANET LORIMER

SADDLEBACK
EDUCATIONAL PUBLISHING

◖QUICKREADS

SERIES 1
Black Widow Beauty
Danger on Ice
Empty Eyes
The Experiment
The Kula'i Street Knights
The Mystery Quilt
No Way to Run
The Ritual
The 75-Cent Son
The Very Bad Dream

SERIES 2
The Accuser
Ben Cody's Treasure
Blackout
The Eye of the Hurricane
The House on the Hill
Look to the Light
Ring of Fear
The Tiger Lily Code
Tug-of-War
The White Room

SERIES 3
The Bad Luck Play
Breaking Point
Death Grip
Fat Boy
No Exit
No Place Like Home
The Plot
Something Dreadful Down Below
Sounds of Terror
The Woman Who Loved a Ghost

SERIES 4
The Barge Ghost
Beasts
Blood and Basketball
Bus 99
The Dark Lady
Dimes to Dollars
Read My Lips
Ruby's Terrible Secret
Student Bodies
Tough Girl

SADDLEBACK
EDUCATIONAL PUBLISHING
www.sdlback.com

Copyright ©2010, 2002 by Saddleback Educational Publishing

ISBN-13: 978-1-61651-207-1
ISBN-10: 1-61651-207-5
eBook: 978-1-60291-929-7

Printed in Guangzhou, China
0911/CA21101490

15 14 13 12 11   2 3 4 5 6

■ ■ ■

Alex stared as the huge green waves rose like sea monsters before crashing to the sand in pools of foam. Their thunder beat against her ears.

She had always loved listening to the thunder of the waves. The rhythm was strangely hypnotic. But today she also heard another sound—one that had haunted her for months. It was the scream of grinding, tearing metal. Soon it grew so loud that it drowned out the noise of the waves.

Alex clapped her hands over her ears, even though she knew that the horrible sounds were *inside* her head. "Stop, please stop! Those sounds will drive me mad!" she thought miserably.

"Alex. Alexandra!" Alex turned and saw her cousin Miranda gesturing impatiently.

Alex took a deep breath of cool, salty air and started back up the beach. Miranda looked excited. "Good news!" she shouted. "You can rent the cottage!"

Alex gazed at her cousin in surprise. "Really? Just like that?"

Miranda's eyes were sparkling. "It's off-season. Mrs. Hansen was delighted to get a tenant this time of year."

Alex turned to study the small gray cottage next to Miranda's house. It was certainly charming. "But is this what's best for me?" she wondered. "After everything that's happened—"

She felt Miranda's hand on her arm.

"I know you're wondering if this is a wise move," Miranda said. "I think it is. You have to live somewhere while you recuperate. This cottage is as good a place as any. In fact, it's *perfect!* You'll have your privacy—but I'll be close by if you need me." She held up a key.

"Shall we go inside and take a look now?"

Alex nodded.

"The doctor says a lot of walking would do you good," Miranda went on. "You can have the beach all to yourself. This time of year you can walk for miles without seeing a soul! We're close to town, and you can use my car if—"

Miranda broke off too late. Alex's face had crumpled. She burst into tears.

Miranda put her arms around her cousin. "I'm so sorry," she whispered. "That was thoughtless. I can drive you to the store, Alex. Or you can have groceries delivered. You—" She broke off in frustration. "Oh, dear. I just seem to be making it worse, don't I?"

Alex drew back, wiping away her tears. "It's not your fault, Miranda. It's me—just me. It's already been months, but I still can't seem to get over it. People have to deal with tragedies every day. What's wrong with *me?*"

By now, they had almost reached the gray cottage. "There's nothing wrong with you," Miranda said softly. "Nothing that time won't heal. Don't forget that you lost someone who was very dear to you, someone—"

Again she broke off too late. She saw Alex grit her teeth, trying to hold back the tears. As if trying to escape her pain, Alex plunged ahead on the path.

Miranda followed, wondering in despair if Alex would ever be able to talk about it. Alex's fiancé Steven had been killed in the car accident. The doctor said that the sooner Alex faced her loss and talked about it, the sooner she would begin to heal. But Alex showed no signs of even accepting Steven's death.

Alex reached the stairs that led up to the veranda of the cottage. She turned to smile at her cousin. "These stairs will give me plenty of exercise," she said as they started up.

Miranda was glad to change the subject. "Look, Alex. You'll have a fantastic view from here," she said.

Inside the cottage, they moved from room to room looking the place over.

"Mrs. Hansen's cleaning woman will come

in tomorrow morning," Miranda explained. "After that, it's all ready! Everything is here—linens, dishes—"

But Alex wasn't listening. An oil painting over the stone fireplace had caught her attention.

It was the portrait of a handsome young man in his late twenties. He had dark brown hair and green eyes that matched the color of the sea. The handsome young man seemed to be gazing right at her. She could almost hear him saying, "I know all your secrets!" Alex felt a slight shudder run down her spine.

She turned away from the portrait and smiled at her cousin. "Who's the guy in the picture?" she asked.

Miranda shrugged. "I have no idea. Probably someone Mrs. Hansen knows. He's a good-looking guy, huh?"

Then Alex noticed something. For the first time in months, she couldn't hear the sounds in her head.

■ ■ ■

Two days later, Alex moved into the cottage. She brought very little with her. "After the accident, I got rid of many of my things," she told Miranda. "They reminded me of—"

She broke off before mentioning Steven's name.

"I never really knew what happened that day," Miranda said gently. "What led up to . . ." Hoping Alex would continue, she let her words trail away.

Alex turned pale. *"Nothing!* We had an accident. St—St—He's dead!" She burst into tears and ran out of the room.

Miranda slumped back into her chair. "I've got to be patient. The poor girl needs more time," she thought sadly.

When Alex returned, Miranda tried to apologize. Alex stopped her. "No, *I'm* the problem," Alex said in a shaky voice. "I know I've got to face what happened—but I just can't do it right now."

After her cousin left, Alex built a fire in the fireplace. Before long the crackling blaze heated the room. Alex made a cup of tea and carried it into the living room. She curled up in a comfortable armchair and gazed into the flames.

Then something made her look up. The man in the painting seemed to be studying her. Alex looked away. But his green eyes and secretive smile again sent a little chill down her spine.

"Oh, for crying out loud!" she scolded herself. "It's only a picture!"

That night she dreamed she was walking along the beach. Just ahead, she saw the figure of a man, his back turned to her. Something about the man seemed familiar. The next thing she knew she was calling out Steven's name.

She ran toward the man. But just as she reached him, he turned toward her. She was looking into the deep green eyes of the man in the portrait!

Awakening with a start, Alex sat up. The

strange dream had left her shaking from head to toe!

■ ■ ■

Alex went to the kitchen and warmed a cup of milk. She hoped it would help her get back to sleep. While she waited for the milk to heat, she peered out the window. A layer of dark, angry clouds partly masked the moon.

She drank her milk slowly, listening to the wind rise. "Sounds like we're in for a storm," she thought to herself.

She felt a stab of disappointment and sighed. She'd hoped to go for a long walk in the morning. Then she remembered that storms often bring strange and wonderful things to shore. "Maybe I'll find some pretty shells tomorrow," she told herself. "Or some interesting pieces of driftwood." She went back to bed.

When she awoke, Alex was happy to see the sun was shining. After lashing the sea and land for a few hours, the storm had worn itself out.

She had a quick breakfast and then hurried down to the shore. Sure enough, there was lots of driftwood. Bits of pretty shells and pebbles lay tangled in strands of wet seaweed.

Alex followed the line of ocean debris down the beach. Before long, her pockets were filled with treasures. Among other things, she'd found a sand dollar and several pieces of green glass, frosted by the waves.

Then a quick movement made Alex look up. A man stood on the beach about 20 feet away from her, staring out over the water. Why did his face look so familiar? Alex frowned, trying to imagine where she'd met him.

Suddenly, the memory of last night's dream flashed into her mind. Her breath caught in her throat. She tried to steady herself. It couldn't be! And yet—

As if drawn by a magnet, Alex took a step toward the man—then another and another. She'd almost closed the distance between them when he turned. She stopped abruptly, shocked by what she saw. Eyes as green as sea glass gazed into hers. His lips parted in a warm smile, and then—*he vanished!*

For a moment, Alex couldn't believe what had happened. She reached out, stroking the air as if somehow she could *touch* him. But it was useless. He was gone, as surely as if he had never been there at all!

■ ■ ■

Shaken, Alex tore back down the beach to her cousin's house.

Miranda was alarmed to hear Alex's story. "There has to be a logical reason for what you—uh—saw," Miranda said, trying to keep her voice calm.

Alex could tell that Miranda was very worried. "She thinks I'm going crazy," Alex thought to herself.

"Did you have breakfast this morning?" Miranda asked.

Alex almost laughed out loud. "Oh! You think my mysterious stranger is the result of hunger pangs? Sorry to disappoint you,

Miranda. I had a great breakfast."

Miranda shrugged. "Okay, how about this: You said you didn't sleep well last night. Maybe—"

"No," Alex said firmly. "I *did* see a man. It's the same guy who's in the portrait. I just can't explain why he vanished."

"Isn't it possible that you imagined the whole thing?" Miranda asked.

"But why?" Alex asked. "Why would I imagine seeing a stranger instead of—" She froze.

"Instead of Steven?" Miranda suggested gently. She saw Alex wince. "You know what the doctor keeps saying," Miranda went on. "Sooner or later, you've got to face what happened. You have to talk about it."

"You just don't understand—I *can't!*" Alex wailed. She dashed out the door.

As she walked back to her own cottage, Alex sensed that Miranda was watching her from the window. "Maybe she's right," Alex thought miserably. "Maybe I *am* going crazy."

■ ■ ■

Back in the cottage, Alex found an old beach towel and draped it over the portrait. She didn't want to look at that face for a while. She was sure she could sense the green-eyed stranger's disappointment.

"You just have too darn much imagination," she scolded herself. Determined not to think about the man in the portrait, she picked up a book.

But when she forced her thoughts away from the green-eyed man, memories of the accident took their place.

She shuddered. "If only I could tell Miranda the truth," Alex whispered, her eyes filling with tears. But the truth was far too terrible to say out loud. "No, no, I can't. No one must ever learn what *really* happened."

Struggling with her memories, Alex began to pace the length of the room. Soon the walls of the cottage seemed to close in on her. She felt as trapped as a pearl in an oyster shell.

"I need to get back outdoors," Alex thought.

"A good long walk, lots of fresh air—that's what I need!"

She grabbed her jacket and hurried outside. A cold wind was blowing off the ocean. Alex took a deep breath. She had always loved the smell of the sea. The warmth of the sun on her skin and the cool bite of the sea-driven breeze always made her feel happy and free. And she especially loved playing tag with the green, sea-monster waves that crashed and foamed at her feet.

As windy as it was, Alex couldn't resist. She pulled off her shoes and socks, tossing them out of the water's reach.

"I really *might* be crazy," she thought happily as the cold swirling water tickled her ankles. Alex dug her toes into the sand.

Then she was struck with the odd feeling that someone was watching her. Whirling around, she turned and saw—her mysterious stranger.

"You!" Alex cried out.

The man's smile vanished, replaced by a look of fear. He reached out to her.

15

At just that moment, Alex heard Miranda shouting her name. She glanced toward her cousin's house and saw Miranda running toward her. For some reason, she was gesturing frantically. "The *waves!* Alex, look out!" Miranda screamed.

Alex glanced over her shoulder. A monster wave was rearing up behind her. She threw herself forward just as it crashed behind her. But she hadn't jumped far enough. A torrent of icy water swirled about her ankles, rising quickly to her knees.

Alex could feel someone grab her arm as the rising water sucked at her legs. The undertow felt like powerful hands tugging her out to sea.

Fighting against the tide, Alex finally felt the water recede. Then she saw that Miranda was helping her up the beach. After a few steps they both collapsed on the sand.

"You scared me, Alex! I was afraid that wave was going to drag you out to sea," Miranda gasped.

Alex sat up, glancing from side to side.

"Where is he?" she asked.

"Where's who?"

"The man in the picture. Just before you called out, I—" She saw the look of fear and disbelief on Miranda's face.

"Oh, Alex, there was no one on the beach but you," Miranda said.

Alex shook her head. "You're wrong, Miranda. I saw—"

Miranda scrambled to her feet and helped Alex stand up. "Come on, Alex. If we don't get changed, we'll catch a cold," Miranda said as she led Alex away.

Alex's spirits sank. How could she convince Miranda that the green-eyed stranger was real?

■ ■ ■

Later, in Miranda's kitchen, the cousins drank cups of hot cocoa. Miranda didn't have to say a word. Alex knew what was on her cousin's mind.

"You think I'm crazy," Alex said.

Miranda gazed wordlessly at her cousin's

anxious face. "Did it ever occur to you that dwelling on this stranger keeps you from facing Steven's death?" Miranda blurted out. "I think you're falling in love, Alex—falling in love with someone who isn't real—a *ghost!* It's a lot easier than facing the truth!"

Alex turned pale. "How can you say such a thing?" she whispered. "I'm just curious about him. If I only knew who he was—"

"So let's find out," Miranda said. "Once you know who he is, maybe you'll finally be able to move on." She reached for the phone. "I'll call Mrs. Hansen and ask her about the portrait."

Unfortunately, Mrs. Hansen wasn't at home.

"The housekeeper said she left on a business trip this morning," Miranda said as she replaced the receiver. "But there's something else you can do, Alex. Research. Right in town, there's a library and a museum. Maybe you'll find your answer there."

Half an hour later, Miranda drove Alex to the town's small library. "The museum is next door," Miranda said, pointing. "And the town's best coffee shop is on the corner. I'll meet you for coffee in a couple of hours."

■ ■ ■

Settled down in the library, Alex soon found some information on the gray cottage. Mrs. Hansen's father had built the place in the 1940s. The cottage had become a favorite vacation spot for the whole family. Over the years, many of their friends had come to the beach to visit them. But unfortunately, the library had no pictures of either the original family or their friends.

"Try the museum," the librarian said. "The historical society has collected a lot of information about local people. You might have more success there."

Alex told the museum curator how curious she was about the portrait. She said nothing about seeing her mystery man on the beach.

The curator smiled. "I know exactly who you're talking about," he said. "It's a good-looking, dark-haired man with intense green eyes, right?"

Alex nodded eagerly. How did he know that? It was a *perfect* description!

"He was a popular figure in town," the curator went on. "Let me see if I can find a photo of him." He strode quickly into the next room.

"But who is he?" Alex demanded as she hurried to keep up.

"Eric Vandermeer," the curator said, as if the name explained everything. He skimmed through a file drawer of photographs, handing one to Alex. "Is this the man?"

Alex studied the photo and nodded. Eric Vandermeer was indeed her green-eyed stranger. In the picture, he was posed in front of the gray cottage.

She turned the photo over, looking for a date. How could it be? The photo had been taken 50 years ago!

■ ■ ■

Alex had no idea how she found her way to the coffee shop. Miranda was sitting in a booth near the back.

"Alex, are you okay? You look like you've seen a ghost!" Miranda exclaimed.

Alex slid into the booth. "I think I have," she said in a shaky voice.

Over bowls of clam chowder, Alex told her cousin about Eric Vandermeer. "He was Mrs. Hansen's father. That's why his portrait is in the cottage. He died about 15 years ago."

Miranda was fascinated. "Do you know how he died?" she asked.

Alex smiled weakly. "Of old age," she said. "Nothing terrible or at all tragic happened to him. So why would his ghost still be haunting the cottage?"

Miranda shrugged. "I don't know anything about ghosts. I'm not even sure I believe in them. But at least you've solved your mystery. Now that you know who the green-eyed mystery man is, you can move on with your own life!"

"Oh, I'm not so sure about that," Alex thought to herself.

■ ■ ■

The next day Alex asked Miranda if she could borrow her car.

Miranda stared at Alex in surprise. "Borrow my—of course! But why—"

"I need to go back to the library," Alex said, "to get some books to read."

Alex hadn't driven since the accident, but *driving* was no problem for her. "Besides," she thought to herself, "I wasn't the one behind the wheel that day. It isn't driving that upsets me!"

When Alex returned from the library, Miranda hurried out to meet her. "Did you find—" Then she stared at the books Alex held, leaning closer to read the titles. "Ghosts? Hauntings?"

Alex smiled weakly as she handed Miranda the car keys. "Don't worry. I'm just curious, that's all."

Miranda shook her head, looking disappointed. "I thought you were ready to move on," she said sternly.

"I need answers," Alex snapped as Miranda followed her into the house. In the kitchen, she picked up the top book and waved it in Miranda's face.

"I spent the whole morning reading about ghosts," Alex said. "And nothing in these books indicates that what I saw was a phantom!"

Miranda took the book and leafed through it. She stopped at a so-called spirit photograph. "Well, what *do* you think you saw?" she asked.

Alex dropped into a chair. She sighed. "I don't know," she said. "The man I saw was just as solid as you are, Miranda. I couldn't see through him. And he looked right at me!" She frowned, remembering. "That was the first time. The second time I saw him was like a continuation of the first time."

Miranda sat down on the couch across

from Alex. "I'm sorry, Alex. I just don't understand," she said.

"It's hard to explain," Alex said. "It was like watching a piece of film. When the film stopped, he vanished! The second time I saw him, it was like the film picked up where it had left off."

"So, is there *more* to this piece of film?" Miranda asked. "Do you think you'll see Eric again?"

Alex shrugged. "Maybe."

Miranda stood and began to pace. "Alex, I'm *begging* you to stop. This is insane! You came here to heal, not put off the healing! Your doctor told me—"

Alex jumped to her feet. "Stop it!" she yelled. "Leave me alone, Miranda! I'm sick and tired of hearing you hinting that I'm off my rocker!"

She grabbed her jacket and ran out the back door.

Miranda followed. "Alex, please, wait!" Miranda called after her. "I'm really sorry I upset you. I'm just—"

But Alex refused to listen. She buttoned up her jacket and sprinted down the beach.

Miranda ran after her. She was determined to confront her cousin, once and for all. "You've got to stop running away," Miranda called out. "Listen to me, Alex! You can't go on pretending that nothing happened. You can't ignore the fact that Steven is gone."

Alex stopped, turned, and glared at her cousin. Her facial expression was deeply sad—even tortured. "Don't you think I know what happened?" she screamed. "No one knows what happened better than I do!"

"But it wasn't your fault," Miranda shouted. "When will you realize that? What happened wasn't your—"

■ ■ ■

"Oh, but it was!" Alex's face twisted in grief as she remembered. "It was *all* my fault! Steven and I were arguing. That's why he didn't see the other car swerve! If we hadn't been arguing, he could have reacted faster and avoided the accident."

"But you can't blame yourself—" Miranda started to say.

"You don't get it! I was the one who started the fight! *I told Steven I didn't want to marry him!*"

Miranda was stunned. Her mouth dropped open in disbelief. "What?"

Alex nodded. Tears streamed down her cheeks. "Okay, Miranda! You want to know all of the terrible truth?"

Miranda gazed at Alex silently.

"Shortly after we got engaged, I realized I didn't love Steven," Alex sobbed, "but I couldn't say anything. We were the storybook couple. We were supposed to live happily ever after. The trouble was, every time I thought about growing old with Steven, it scared me to death. I felt trapped. Finally, I realized I had to break off the engagement."

"Oh, I'm so sorry," Miranda gasped.

"I felt awful," Alex sobbed. "But I simply couldn't hold it in any longer. Steven was behind the wheel. I should have made him pull over when I told him. But for some reason, it all just spilled out. He was so hurt, so angry!"

"Oh, Alex!" Miranda started to close the distance between them, but Alex backed away.

"Don't come near me!" she yelled. "And don't try to comfort me, Miranda. I don't deserve it! A very good man is dead because of me, because of what I did—"

"No!" Miranda cried out. She meant that Alex must stop blaming herself. But before she could explain, she saw what Alex did not. Like an immense green wall of death, a gigantic wave was rising up behind her cousin. *"No!"* Miranda screamed.

Alex stumbled back even farther. Too late she felt the giant wave crash over her, knocking her off her feet. The wall of icy water choked her, deafened her, tossed her about like a rag doll. Then the undercurrent tugged at her, sucking her away from the safety of the shore.

Suddenly, strong arms reached out from nowhere. Alex could feel someone was lifting her from the raging surf and gently placing her on the sand.

When she caught her breath, Alex opened her eyes, blinking against the sting of the salt water. At first, all she could see was a dark silhouette. Then the figure leaned closer and a face came into focus.

Alex gasped. She was gazing into the eyes of—*her mystery man.*

■ ■ ■

"**E**ric, it's you!" Alex exclaimed, reaching up to touch his cheek. He didn't vanish at her touch. Instead, he grinned.

"Michael," he said. "Michael Hansen."

Alex struggled to sit up. She could see her cousin hovering right behind him. "See, Miranda, he's *not* a ghost!" she whispered hoarsely.

Miranda tried to smile through her confusion. "I'll get some towels," she said.

Michael smiled at Alex. "No, you were *my* ghost," he said. "It was so strange. I was sitting at my computer and then suddenly, there you were! But the next second you were gone."

With Michael's help, Alex climbed to her feet. "I thought I was going crazy," she said shakily.

Michael laughed. "So did I!"

They slowly climbed the stairs to the cottage. After hot showers, Alex and Michael exchanged stories about seeing each other. "I don't understand," Alex said. "How could we see ghost-like visions of each other?"

Michael laughed. "As a science-fiction writer," he explained, "I think I just might know what happened to us." Then, as Alex and Miranda listened, he described what he called a *time slip*.

■ ■ ■

Michael took a piece of string and laid it on the table. Then he bent it into a U shape. "Imagine that time doesn't run in a straight line," he said. "If time is flexible—like this string—it can turn in on itself." To demonstrate, he pushed the two sides of the U together until they touched. "In theory, they say it's possible that when two time frames touch, a door between them opens. That may be one way to explain ghosts! In our case, the door opened into our future."

"But how did you know to come here today?" Alex asked.

Michael grinned. "Funny thing about that," he said. "I never come down here. But before my mother—your landlady— went out of town, she asked me to make sure everything was okay. Today I had an overpowering urge to make that trip!"

He glanced up at the towel-draped portrait. "I take it you didn't like my grand-father staring down at you," he went on in a teasing voice.

"Your *grandfather!*" Alex exclaimed.

Then, feeling a great weight lift from her shoulders, Alex laughed. Now that she'd confessed the truth to Miranda, she no longer blamed herself for Steven's death. "I guess *Steven* was my ghost," she thought to herself. "Now that I've let him go, I really can go on."

Michael gazed intently into Alex's eyes. "And now that you know I'm not a ghost—do I stand a chance of getting to know you better?"

Alex grinned wickedly. "At least the *ghost* of a chance," she said.

After-Reading Wrap-Up

1. Did you like the title of the story? Why or why not? Think of another possible title.

2. Why is Miranda important to the story? What *purpose* does her character serve?

3. Who was the young man in the portrait?

4. What did Alex learn from her experiences?

5. How did the young man in the picture die?

6. Reread the description of a "time slip." Now use your imagination and write a paragraph describing a "time slip" situation.